For Dieter, Clara, Angela and Lilian

British Library Cataloguing in Publication Data
Brown, Ruth
   The world that Jack built.
   1. Pollution
   I. Title
   363.7'3

   ISBN 0-86264-269-8

This book has been printed on acid-free paper

© 1990 by Ruth Brown.
First published in Great Britain in 1990 by Andersen Press Ltd., 20 Vauxhall Bridge Road, London SW1V 2SA.
Published in Australia by Random House Australia Pty., 20 Alfred Street, Milsons Point, Sydney NSW 2061.
All rights reserved. Colour separated by Photolitho AG Offsetreproduktionen, Gossau, Zürich, Switzerland.
Printed in Italy by Grafiche AZ, Verona.

3   4   5   6   7   8   9

The World
that Jack Built

Ruth Brown

Andersen Press • London

This is the house that Jack built.

These are the trees that grow by the house that Jack built.

This is the stream that flows past the trees, that grow by the house that Jack built.

These are the meadows which border the stream, which
flows past the trees, that grow by the house that Jack built.

These are the woods that shelter the meadows, that border
the stream, which flows past the trees, that grow by the
house that Jack built.

These are the hills which form the valley, that surrounds the woods,
that shelter the meadows, which border the stream, that
flows past the trees, that grow by the house that Jack built.

These are the hills that form the valley next to the one that protects
the woods, that shelter the meadows, which border the stream, that
flows past the trees, that grow by the house that Jack built.

And these are the woods which cover those hills —

and shelter the meadows —

which border the stream –

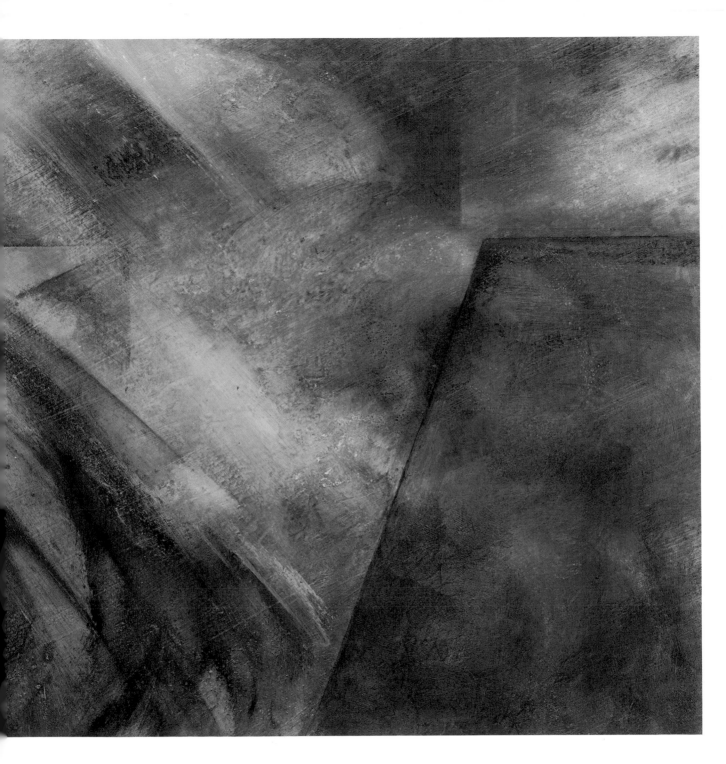

that flows past the place where the trees used to grow –

next to the factory that Jack built.